THE CLOTH OF DREAMS

THE CLOTH OF DREAMS

Fairy Tales for Young Children

Edited by
SALLY GRINDLEY

Illustrated by
JAMES MAYHEW

LITTLE, BROWN AND COMPANY
Boston · Toronto · London

Editor's dedication: *For Randall and Tom*
Illustrator's dedication: *For Mari de Salvi*

The Dragon Brothers © 1992 by W.J. Corbett
Hilda Mathilda © 1992 by Joyce Dunbar
A Length of White Satin © 1992 by Adèle Geras
The Boy and the Fish © 1992 by Sally Grindley
Mr Midnight's Tree Bird © 1992 by Sarah Hayes
Léonie and the Last Wolf © 1992 by Mary Hoffman
The Cloth of Dreams © 1992 by Jenny Koralek
The Palace Made out of Glass © 1992 by James Mayhew
The Last Wish in the World © 1992 by Chris Powling
Tommy the Rhymer © 1992 by Leon Rosselson

First published in Great Britain in 1992 by
Little, Brown and Company (UK) Ltd
165 Great Dover Street, London SE1 4YA

ISBN 0–316–88901–6
A CIP catalogue record for this book is available from
the British Library

Designed by Janet James

Typeset by DP Photosetting, Aylesbury, Bucks
Colour separations by Fotographics, Hong Kong
Printed and bound in Italy by Amilcare Pizzi

CONTENTS

THE CLOTH OF DREAMS

Jenny Koralek

There was once a boy who was getting ready to visit his grandmother, when he tripped on his cloth of dreams and tore it. His grandmother had made the cloth of dreams and spread it over his cradle when he was born.

"It will keep the dark night things away," she said to his mother, "but only, of course, until he is big enough to forge his own courage."

Thanks to the cloth of dreams the boy had never yet known a bad night, but there it now lay with two large holes in it.

"Never mind," said his mother. "Give it to your grandmother and she will most surely mend it."

But when the boy got to his grandmother's house he forgot all about the torn cloth of dreams.

In the garden the swing was waiting for him under the apple tree, the doves were calling to be fed, the goldfish were blowing bubbles in the lilypond and the sundial was telling him it was supper time.

In the kitchen the table creaked with all his favourite food, salty and spicy, sugary and sweet, hot and cold and fizzy. In the bedroom the pillows were punchy, the mattress was bouncy and when he drew

the cloth of dreams up to his chin, his grandmother lit a candle and told him the kind of stories he liked best, stories with rhyme and without reason.

So of course the boy forgot all about the torn cloth of dreams. But his grandmother had seen the holes and, as she made her way to her room, smiled sadly to herself.

When the boy fell asleep with moonlight on his face, a chain of nightmares came out through the holes in the cloth of dreams and, as they were new to him, he was quite helpless in front of them.

A frightful hag chased him through a wood full of leafless trees with branches like claws and caught him and tickled him with long, stabbing, bony fingers. He pulled himself away, but no sooner was he free than he fell into the jaws of a huge fish. Down he fell into its hot, steamy belly, which was so big the boy could stand up in it. He shouted and shouted for his grandmother but no sounds came out of his mouth. When at last the fish opened its toothy jaws the boy fell out with a crash and landed on a frozen puddle.

Suddenly he woke up and found he was lying on the floor shivering with the torn cloth of dreams beside him. Then he remembered the holes and what his mother had said to him: "Give it to your grandmother and she will most surely mend it."

So the boy picked up the cloth of dreams and opened the door of his bedroom. But oh! how dark the landing was, how big and dark. The moon had disappeared behind a huge cloud, his grandmother had taken the candle with her and if there were other lights the boy did not know how to find them. He could see the light glowing beneath his grandmother's door, but that only made things worse because he could make out shapes all round him, uncertain shapes which might be the things that were there in the day but might be things which came in the night.

The boy was afraid to turn back and afraid to go on. His body trembled and his teeth chattered but he fixed his eyes on the glow from his grandmother's room and set forth with his fears across the dark, shape-filled landing. He stubbed his toes on one strange thing and hit his elbow on another. Each step he took made a fearful creak, something sighed in the curtains and for a moment he lost sight of the light.

But suddenly he was there in the doorway of his grandmother's glowing room, holding out the torn cloth of dreams.

"Horrible things came through these holes," he said, "and I made a dark crossing to come to you. Please will you mend it?"

"With your help," said his grandmother, "I most surely will."

And she picked up an empty basket and led him to a little door that he had not seen before and set him on a steep stairway.

"You must fetch me threads from the sun and threads from the moon," said his grandmother.

"B–but," stammered the boy.

"No buts," said his grandmother. "I am too old to climb the stairs."

Gripped with fear the boy climbed the stairs one by one and came out onto a flat place on the roof which seemed to be touching the sky. The silver moon was fading into a green sky and the golden sun was rising into a rosy sky and the boy had never before seen anything so beautiful and powerful, so quiet and so certain. All the same he was terrified. Surely the sun would burn him. Surely the moon would freeze him. But surely his grandmother would not let harm come to him. After all, it was she who had made the cloth of dreams to protect him.

So the boy put out a brave hand and pulled at the sun's first rays, which he found were as warm as his grandmother's smile. Then he pulled at the moon's last rays, which he found to be as cold and as sharp as his fears in the dark, but he went on standing there firmly in his bare feet, pulling at the rays until the basket was full. Then he bounded down the stairs and gave it to his grandmother.

In the twinkling of an eye she threaded the gold and threaded the silver and flashed her needle through the cloth of dreams and suddenly the gaping holes had disappeared.

"There you are," said his grandmother, holding out the cloth of dreams. "Not that you need it now. Tonight you have forged your own courage. Now you are your own true sword and will know how to do battle with night and day and light and dark and smiles and frowns and fears and joys."

"Will I?" asked the boy in a whisper.

"You will," said his grandmother.

And they smiled at one another.

Then, as the world was stepping out of night into a new day, the boy ran downstairs two at a time, out into the garden and across the dewy grass. Onto the swing he jumped and swung it high, higher than he ever had before.

THE PALACE MADE OUT OF GLASS

James Mayhew

The Princess of the East was very rich and had nearly everything a five-year-old Princess could possibly want – except an imagination. But her mother and father, who were a King and Queen of course, didn't think their daughter, who was called Clarissa, should have one.

"Dangerous things," said the King. "Children always imagine things in the wrong way and get into all sorts of trouble." The Queen nodded wisely, and so that was that.

On the other side of the river, in the West, there lived another Princess, called Melissa. She was not rich, for although her parents were also a King and Queen, they had spent all of their money building a palace out of glass.

It had seemed a nice idea at the time, and it truly was a lovely palace. But it was not really very practical.

It was always cold, because the central heating made the walls crack. And there was a law against tripping over ever since the royal nursemaid fell and smashed an entire floor with her nose. But Melissa loved the palace more than anything and she didn't mind being poor and not having toys or dolls one little bit. But then she had a good imagination – her Fairy Godmother had given it to her for a Christening present, in a little box – so she could easily pretend she was the richest Princess in all the world.

Hour upon hour she would dream dreams and tell tales to herself, in the cut glass towers, or in the royal gardens. When the evening sunlight fell onto the lake, it cast reflections onto the palace that made it look as if it had been made out of gold. And at night, when the sky was full of diamonds, the moonlight made the palace look like mother-of-pearl. Princess Melissa was very happy.

Until she heard from her mother about how rich the Princess Clarissa was. Then she started to use her imagination in the wrong way and tried to think of what it must be like to be really rich, instead of just pretend rich. She thought of all the toys and dolls, and in the end she went to see the Princess Clarissa.

"How would you like to live in a palace of gold, with a sky full of diamonds above?" she said.

"I must have it for my birthday," said Clarissa, impressed. "How much is it?" She was rather spoilt and used to having what she wanted.

"Not for sale," said Melissa. "Might swap with this place though – plus contents."

"Agreed," said the King and the Queen of the East. And Melissa took them West, over the river, to the palace made out of glass.

"But this isn't gold," said the King.

"Where are the diamonds?" asked the Queen.

"You've tricked us," said Clarissa.

"Oh, for goodness sake," said Melissa, stomping up the glass steps. "You have to have some imagination." And she was in such a temper that she put her imagination into the box it had come in, and gave it to Princess Clarissa.

Almost at once, Princess Clarissa saw things differently. She stood at the door and watched the sunset.

"Isn't it lovely?" she said. "I can't decide if it looks like liquid gold, or pure silk, or fruit trifle." And she ran off to explore her new home. Her poor parents just scratched their heads in wonder.

Meanwhile, Melissa went to live in the other palace. She wore the fine clothes, and ate jellies, drank lemonade, and lived a life of luxury.

She played with the toys and dolls until they were all broken. She read the books until she knew them all by heart. In no time at all she was bored, because now that she didn't have any imagination, there was nothing to do. She called her Fairy Godmother up on the telephone to ask her advice.

"Sometimes it's better to dream about something, than actually have it," said the Fairy Godmother. "You'll have to ask Clarissa to swap back."

But Clarissa loved the palace made out of glass more than anything, now that she had an imagination. She didn't want to swap back. Melissa wept and screamed.

"Oh look!" said Clarissa. "How clever you are, you can make pearls come out of your eyes." Clarissa never cried because she was so happy.

But one night Clarissa had a terrible dream. She wasn't really used to having an imagination, and she wasn't sure how to use it

properly. She had made the moonlit shadows look like witches, and now they wouldn't go away.

The next morning she went back to her old home to see Melissa.

"Please show me how to use the imagination properly," she said.

"Only if you give it back, and the palace of glass as well," said Melissa.

"But then I won't be able to make things up any more," said Clarissa.

"Well, I'll let you keep a tiny bit, if you'll swap back," said Melissa. "What do you say?"

"I suppose that's fair," said Clarissa, who was a reasonable child (and knew a bargain when she heard one). And so they swapped back.

Now the two of them are the very best of friends, and they dream dreams and tell each other tales all day long. Melissa has shown Clarissa how to use her imagination properly, and they only think up nice things. They are both very careful not to use their imaginations in the wrong way.

They like to play at the palace made out of glass most of all. They are probably there right now. I expect they are sitting beside the lake trying as hard as possible to imagine it is the never-ending ocean, and that there is a casket of gold, right at the bottom, guarded by an emerald sea-dragon.

HILDA MATHILDA

Joyce Dunbar

There was once a poor farmworker who had a daughter called Hilda Mathilda. Life was very hard for them and they had to skimp and save for a living.

Luckily, there was a young farmer nearby who thought Hilda Mathilda was a fine, pretty girl and one day he said, "Will you marry me, Hilda Mathilda?"

"Yes," said Hilda Mathilda, and she moved from the humble farmworker's hovel into a splendid farmhouse full of good things.

They had not been married a day when the young farmer had to be away on business.

"I will leave you to manage things," he said to Hilda Mathilda and he thought how fortunate he was to have a wife who had learnt to manage things carefully instead of a wife who would spend all his money.

When her husband had gone, Hilda Mathilda looked at herself in the mirror, at her beautiful dress of rose silk. She wasn't used to wearing such things.

"This dress is much too pretty to wear," said she. "Off with it!"

Well, when the dress heard that it went flouncing across the meadow until it met a donkey who thought it was just the thing to wear, and he put it on.

21

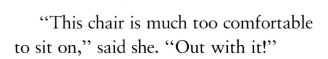

Hilda Mathilda put on her old grey calico dress and sat down for a moment in a chair. She wasn't used to sitting on such things.

"This chair is much too comfortable to sit on," said she. "Out with it!"

Well, when the chair heard that it went rushing off down the lane until it met a dog who thought it was just the thing to sit on and he sat on it.

Hilda Mathilda put out a stool instead and went about the house.

It wasn't long before the china went the same way as the chair, and the rugs went the same way as the china, and the curtains went the same way as the rugs. As for the fire, it just didn't get lit.

At supper time Hilda Mathilda looked in the pantry to see what there was to eat. There was a pork pie and pheasant and some eggs. There was cake and strawberries and cream. She wasn't used to eating such things.

"This food is much too good to eat," said Hilda Mathilda. "Away with it!"

Well, when the food heard that it went scrambling about in the fields where it met a whole lot of mice who thought it was just the stuff to eat, and they ate it all.

Hilda Mathilda laid the table with bread and cheese instead and went to see what there was to drink. She found a flagon of rich red wine. She wasn't used to drinking such stuff.

"This wine is much too good to drink," she said. "Be gone with it!"

Well, when the wine heard that it ran off into the town until it met a vagabond who thought it was just the stuff to drink and he drank it all.

Hilda Mathilda put out a jug of water instead and waited for her husband to come home.

After his hard day of business the young farmer was tired and
hungry. He was looking forward to a good supper by the fire with
his pretty new wife.

But what did he find when he got home?

Hilda Mathilda in an old grey calico dress.

A farmhouse that looked like a hovel.

"Where is the rose silk dress I gave you?"
asked the husband.

"Much too pretty to wear," said
Hilda Mathilda.

"Where is my favourite armchair?"
asked the husband.

"Much too comfortable to sit on,"
said Hilda Mathilda.
"Where is the pork pie and the pheasant and the eggs?
Where is the cake and the cream?" asked the husband.

24

"Much too good to eat," said Hilda Mathilda.

"Where is my flagon of wine?" asked the husband.

"Much too good to drink," said Hilda Mathilda.

Well, the husband didn't ask any more questions because he knew what the answer would be. He scratched his head instead and wondered what to do about such a simpleton of a wife.

"Hilda Mathilda," he said at last, "I see you have managed very well. Let us sit down now on these stools by this cold grate and have our supper of bread and cheese and water."

And they did.

"Hilda Mathilda," said the husband when he had finished, "I am sure you are as tired as I am. Let's go to bed."

And they went upstairs.

"Hilda Mathilda," said the husband as they were about to lie down on the enormous bed, "I am sure this bed is much too soft to sleep on. We must sleep on the stone cold floor."

And they tried.

"Hilda Mathilda," said the husband after a while, "I am sure we are much too tired to sleep so we must round up the sheep instead."

So they spent the cold wet night rounding up sheep and got home in the morning very dirty. Hilda Mathilda ran a hot bath.

"Hilda Mathilda," said her husband, "that water is much too clean to get washed in," and he emptied the ash from the grate into it and some coals. Then they both had a very dirty bath.

Outside, the sun was shining and the birds were singing.

"This is much too fine a day to enjoy," said the husband. "Let's go to bed."

And they did, on the stone cold floor. They slept all day and all night.

When Hilda Mathilda woke up in the morning, she ached in every bone of her body. She was sooty from head to foot.

"Why!" said her husband. "There is a warm bath all ready and waiting. What shall we do with it, Hilda Mathilda?"

"Get washed in it," said she.

"Bless my soul!" said the husband when she had finished her bath. "There is a blue muslin dress laid out. What shall you do with it, Hilda Mathilda?"

"Wear it," said she.

"Good gracious!" said the husband when she had put on her dress. "There is a good breakfast prepared, on a fine linen tablecloth, with fine china. What shall we do with it, Hilda Mathilda?"

"Enjoy it," said she.

"Enjoy it," said he, "and be grateful."

And they did. They made it a celebration breakfast. The fire was lit in the grate and the donkey came in the rose silk dress and the dog came on the best armchair and the mice who had eaten all the food came and the vagabond who had drunk all the wine came and the china and the rugs and the curtains came and they all had a splendid time. And Hilda Mathilda was very happy.

THE DRAGON BROTHERS

W. J. Corbett

One stormy night in the Magic Forest the dragons found a baby under a bush. He was wrapped in a cloak and crying bitterly. Beside him lay a lady, her face white in death.

"The unknown lady is at peace," said the first dragon, pity in his eyes. "But the child still clings to life. Let us take him home and raise him as our own. He will be company for our pride and joy."

"I agree," said his wife, breathing warm air over their find. "If we can raise one son to become big and strong we can surely raise two. But handle the child gently, for he's already precious to me."

Then with a gentle nose she scraped a grave and buried the poor lady under the bush where she had died. And the storm dashed blue rose petals from the bush onto the mound of earth as if to mourn the dead mother.

Back home in the cave the baby was unwound from the sodden cloak and fed a rich broth of mushrooms and milk and healing herbs. Then he was tucked into the nest, where he fell quickly to sleep, lulled by a dragon lullaby that grieved for all sons who must die because dragons and humans could not live together in peace.

The flickering glow from the ever-burning fire lit up the cave. The walls were hung with gold and jewels and the booty of battles hoarded down the centuries, for dragons prized such things. The fire also illuminated the finger-ring strung around the baby's neck on a twist of twine, its blue-rose emblem stirring great troubles in the hearts of the dragons. For it was the ring of a prince, of a dragon-slayer. But because they loved their new son completely the dragons stifled their fears, refusing to see future danger in the face of an innocently sleeping child.

The dragon brothers grew big and strong. Many happy days they spent playing together in the sunny glades of the Magic Forest. Small animals and birds would flee in alarm when the brothers staged their mock duels.

"Beware my glittering sword lest it should pierce your heart, wicked dragon," the boy would cry, brandishing a blackthorn stick.

"Take care I don't burn you to a crisp with my fiery breath, puny human," his brother would roar, advancing in all his hugeness.

When dusk fell over the Magic Forest the tired but happy brothers would return to the cave for their favourite meal of mushrooms and milk and healing herbs. And the seasons turned, bringing new years.

One stormy night in the Magic Forest, when the dragon family were warm and dry in their cave, the parents called their sons to the ever-burning fire. Their anguish was plain in the flickering light as they spoke to their now-grown sons.

"It is time," wept the wife to her dragon son. "Gaze into the flames and see your destiny. I turn my face for you must read it, not I."

The puzzled young dragon stared into the glowing embers and saw the pictures flaring, hissing and sighing before his eyes. And his mind was filled with a terrible truth. Without a word to parent or brother he shambled out into the storm that raged through the Magic Forest. He did not look back.

"Equally loved son," said the dragon, turning to the bewildered dragon boy, "now you must gaze into the fire and see your destiny.

And when you turn and leave for ever, never turn your heart on us, your loving parents."

Their son, now a sturdy young man, gazed into the fire as he was told. And there he saw the wicked King, his mother in desperate flight from the castle, her baby in her arms. He saw her fall, exhausted, in the Magic Forest, and a great anger swelled in him.

"Take these as your protection and your birthright," said his father, his eyes filled with pain. "And if you can spare one life in your righteous quest, be a loving and forgiving brother." Reaching out, he took from the glittering wall a bright, sharp sword and buckled it about his son. Reaching again, he took the cloak they had found their baby in. As the folds fell from their son's shoulders, revealed was the blue-rose emblem adorning it. Squeezing his hands in tenderness, her clawed paws trembling, his weeping mother slipped the blue-rose ring on his finger. The duty they had feared to face was complete. The dragon parents had lost their sons. Cruel destiny had snatched them away.

"Like your brother, never look back," they cried as their second son strode out of the cave into the storm-tossed Magic Forest.

The dragon boy paused in the Magic Forest. As the lightning flashed, he knelt at the grave of his mother under the blue-rose bush. Then he stood up and strode out of the trees and onto the plain beyond, his eyes looking up at the castle on the hill . . . the Blue-Rose Castle of his father, and of his fathers before. Drawing his bright, sharp sword he marched up the hill to avenge the death of his mother, and to take back that which was his by right. But his brave heart sank when he saw the keeper of the gate, the enemy who barred his way. Roaring fiercely and breathing fire was his dragon brother, acting out his own destiny, but with a heavy heart.

Brother gazed at beloved brother. Both remembered their childhood games. How could such close brothers forget those happy days in the sunny glades of the Magic Forest and kill each other? Could either brother slay the one he loved best in the world? The two

brothers continued to stare at each other, their thoughts confused, their emotions torn.

"I command you, dragon, burn the usurper with your fiery breath," cried the wicked, cowering King. "As my slave and keeper of my gate I order you to be rid of this impudent Prince for ever."

"I cannot kill this one, for he's my brother," wailed the broken-hearted dragon.

"And I would sooner break my sword and die," cried the Prince, weeping. "Oh, my brother, that destiny should bring us both to this."

Back home in the cave their saddened parents gazed into the ever-burning fire. Then pictures began to flicker, images that brought great joy to their grieving hearts. Suddenly, there were their beloved sons advancing side by side to slay and scatter the wicked King and his court. Then, together as brothers, they entered the Blue-Rose Castle to the loud "Hurrahs" of the happy people. The Prince of the Blue-Rose was home.

"Thus let it be," sighed the dragon parents in their warm cave in the Magic Forest. "The love of our sons has made a mockery of destiny. Now we can rest content."

And the storm abated in the Magic Forest and the blue-rose bush grew strong to shed never-ending petals onto the grave of a lady who had not died in vain.

THE BOY AND THE FISH

Sally Grindley

He came every day to the same spot, a small tousle-haired, bright-eyed boy. He sat by the low bridge, behind him a mess of old warehouses and empty wharf buildings, forgotten edges of the city. He sat quietly for hours, occasionally plucking fresh maggots from his tin and recasting his line. It didn't seem to worry him that the fish didn't bite. He would gaze at the light playing hide-and-seek with shadows on the water. An occasional heron would loiter knee-deep close by, a fellow fisher but far more successful. This was a magical place.

He had often seen the old lady sitting under the bridge. He wondered if she lived there, among her bulging bundles and bags. She would smile at him and laugh to herself a lot. Then she started wandering over to ask if he had caught anything. He wished she wouldn't. Although it didn't worry him if he didn't catch anything, he didn't like having to tell her that he wasn't very good at fishing. Besides, he preferred to be on his own. Home was crowded with noise. Here it was peaceful.

It wasn't long before she had asked him what he thought about while he fished. And he had told her that he dreamed of catching a huge silver carp, and bringing it in after a big struggle, and taking it home to show his brothers and sisters.

Then one day the old lady said to the boy, "I can make the fish jump." The boy looked at her in astonishment, and then, feeling rather embarrassed because the poor thing was obviously batty, said, "Can you?"

Before he could say anything else, he was blinded by myriad flashes of silver and gold and brilliant pinks, greens, purples and blues. Hundreds of fish leapt and danced and twisted and turned in front of him. Dozens landed in his keep net, while dozens more fell back into the water only to leap again, higher and higher, in an aerobatic display that left the boy gasping with wonder.

Then all was quiet. "But how – ?" said the boy.

"Don't ask," said the old woman. "And don't tell. It's a secret. A very special memory to keep to yourself." She smiled and went back to her seat under the bridge.

That afternoon the boy was late home, so heavy and difficult to carry was his keep net full of fish. When he emptied them out before his brothers and sisters, he forgot all about what the old woman had said. Seeing their startled faces, he couldn't help boasting about how he had discovered the secret of catching fish, and how he had landed them all by himself, one by one. For supper that evening, eleven hungry mouths settled down to the most delicious feast of fresh fish cooked over a big open fire, and the boy felt pleased that there were no more jokes about what a hopeless fisherboy he was.

The next day, the boy sat down as usual by the low bridge with its background of derelict buildings. He opened his tin of maggots, fastened one to the hook, cast his line and waited. But something had changed. The fish didn't bite and now he couldn't help feeling irritated.

The old woman seemed to be asleep amongst her bags under the bridge. The boy wondered whether he should wake her. Surely she wouldn't mind making the fish jump for him once more? He crept over to her and shook her gently by the shoulder. She seemed to know who it was before she opened her eyes, and she knew what he wanted.

"Look to the river, but do not spoil what you see there by letting it spoil what you most enjoy."

The boy looked and once again saw big and small fish, narrow and wide fish, fat and flat fish, leaping from the water, soaring into the air, diving, swooping, swerving, until he was dazzled by the sunlight bouncing back off their glistening scales and could see no more. Then all was quiet and the boy found that, as before, his keep net was full of fish.

At home, that evening, the boy described for a second time how he had managed to catch the fish all by himself. And he basked in the praise heaped upon him by his astonished brothers and sisters.

When he reached the bridge the following day, he sat in the usual place, but he couldn't be bothered to cast his line. There seemed little point any more. The old lady was reading to herself. She didn't look at the boy. Soon he grew tired of sitting and wandered over to her.

"Not fishing, today?" she said, without looking up.

"I never catch anything," he said, "so what's the point?"

"You used to enjoy trying," said the old lady. "You used to enjoy that more than anything else."

The boy didn't answer. Then he said: "Do you think you could make the fish jump for me just once more, please? I won't ask again."

"They are jumping now," said the old lady.

The boy looked to the river, but could see nothing more than a spent can and a mess of putrid weed floating by. He stared hard, then turned back to the old lady and asked nervously, "Where are they?"

"They are there," said the old lady, "but you cannot see them any more. By cheating you have lost sight of what you most enjoyed and spoiled the very special memory I gave you."

For weeks after that, the boy came to the river and sat under the bridge, deep in thought. The old lady had gone, so had her bundles and bags. He missed her company and wondered if he would ever see her again.

Then, one day, the desire to fish flooded back. The boy made ready his line, cast it into the water, and a tide of relief swept over him. He sat for hours watching the ripples playing across the water as fish nosed their way to the surface and dived away without biting. In the days that followed, he gradually regained the feeling of quiet contentment that fishing had always given him.

What is more, he nursed a very special memory that grew clearer and clearer as each day passed. One afternoon, just when he was beginning to feel that if he looked hard enough he would see the fish jumping again, his line pulled tight. The boy stood firm and began to wind it in as fast as he could. As he struggled he saw the fins of a large fish tearing through the water's surface before disappearing below. He fought with all his might to pull the line in, until, at last, a huge silver carp catapulted out of the water and spun helplessly from the hook.

The boy's face glowed with pride as he dropped the carp into his keep net and began to haul it home. And as he passed by one of the abandoned wharf buildings, he felt sure he heard someone laughing.

THE LAST WISH IN THE WORLD

Chris Powling

No-one noticed the wizard come out of the subway. He was only a small wizard, after all, with a crumpled hat and a cloak so old its moon and stars were almost invisible.

Besides, it was rush-hour. When it was rush-hour in Skyscraper City who cared about anyone who wasn't in a hurry?

As the wizard paused on a street corner, knees and elbows jostled him and he was hissed at by hard, cross voices. "Shift yourself, fella!"

"Did you rent the whole pavement?"

"Move it, chum."

"I'm sorry," he said. "D'you think . . . is there someone who . . . does anybody . . . ?" But they'd gone before he got the question out.

The wizard edged into a doorway. All afternoon snow had been falling – drifting down and down into icy, traffic-bound streets. "Can it possibly happen here?" the wizard frowned. "Here in the city? When I've failed everywhere else?"

He reached beneath his cloak for the box.

It was a flat, tuck-under-your armpit sort of box, too tatty for jewels and too tinny for cash. But one look at it, one proper look, told you for sure it held a secret – some strange secret.

The wizard heard a cough. He peered round the doorway at a baglady huddled over a grating. "Any spare change, chief?" she winked.

"None at all, I'm afraid. But I have . . . I have got this. Would you like it?"

"A box?"

"With a wish inside, yes. See, it's here on the label: 'On Offer. The Last Wish in the World. Guaranteed to Come True.' Being a wizard, I'm disqualified from wishing, of course. But you can have it for free."

The baglady shrugged. "All wishes are free, chief. And all of them let you down, believe me."

"Not this one. You see . . ."

"Shove off, chief."

Shocked, the wizard tried someone else straightaway. Parked close by was a sleek, elegant limousine. The owner was sleek and elegant, too. One nod to his chauffeur and the rear window slid down soundlessly. "Something there for me?" he snapped.

"This box," said the wizard. "It doesn't look much, I know. But inside is a wish. It's the Last Wish in the World. It'll bring you anything you want, I promise. And I *do* mean . . ."

"Anything?" sniffed the man in the limousine. "You think there's anything left I haven't got?"

"Please . . ." Already the window was sliding up.

The wizard felt a hand on his shoulder. "You on some kind of scam?" came a voice.

"A scam?"

"That's what I said." The cop was looking him up and down with weary, seen-it-all eyes. "What's in the box?" he asked.

"A wish, officer. It's . . ."

"Yeah, I know. It's the Last Wish in the World. And you're not allowed to use it because you're a wizard. I heard you just now. Could this wish of yours bust every crime in the city?"

"Of course."

"Fine," said the cop. "So let's start by busting your crime – the crime you're NOT going to commit, okay? As of now that box of yours stays inside your cloak . . . or the only wish you'll be making, kiddo, is that you never met me. Catch my drift?"

"I do," said the wizard, sadly.

After that, he wandered the streets for a while, his mouth watering a little outside the smart, candle-lit restaurants and his eyes gaping wide at the treasure stacked in every shop window. "Such luxury!" he murmured. "Eager to lap you up . . ."

Well, some of the city was.

He also passed sour-smelling alleyways and vacant lots so dismal even the snow seemed to hate having settled there. ". . . or maybe spit you out," added the wizard with a shudder.

By now he was outside Skyscraper College. "A professor!" he exclaimed. "Someone who thinks a bit deeper. That's who I need." Almost at once he saw one crossing the courtyard, her gown billowing behind her. Was she coming from an evening lecture?

She listened to him carefully, twice over. Then she nodded. "Guaranteed to come true, you say? Now that *is* interesting. Call on me tomorrow after class. We'll discuss it."

"But professor . . ."

"Tomorrow," she said firmly.

The wizard was ready to give up. What had he expected from a place like this? Wasn't the city just a last resort? Anyway, who was there left to ask?

As it happened, a couple on honeymoon. They were outside the park, in a horse-drawn buggy for tourists, when he approached. "A

wish?" said the wife. "Bound to come true? Who needs it when we've got each other?"

But the husband smiled. "Here," he said. "We don't mean to be rude, sir. Take this – maybe it'll cheer you up!" Before the wizard could refuse, the buggy had moved off, its bells jingling in the darkness. He stared at the money he'd been given. "A profit?" he said in dismay. "Now I'm making a profit?"

That clinched it.

Wearily, he began the long trudge back to the subway. "Doesn't anyone believe in magic any more?" he sighed. "No wonder the world is down to its last wish. It'll die out altogether if . . ."

He stopped suddenly in his tracks. "Wait, though. Maybe I should turn it loose myself and see what happens." Already he had a smile on his face.

With the young man's tip, he hired a spade from a street sweeper. He was laughing so much as he piled up snow alongside the subway that people on their way to theatres and cinemas crossed the street to avoid him.

Soon the snowman was finished. It was shaped like a wizard from its crumpled hat to its cloak faintly traced with a moon and stars. He put the box in the fold of its arms.

ON OFFER

THE LAST WISH IN THE WORLD

GUARANTEED TO COME TRUE

The wizard stepped back in the shadows.

A few kids, with their minds on sledges and snowball fights, perhaps, paid no attention at all as they passed.

Then the girl arrived.

Probably she should have been tucked up in bed. Certainly her clothes were too skimpy for weather as bad as this – though her eyes sparkled from the fun of it. She liked the look of the snowman at

once. When she spotted the box, its strangeness made her catch her breath. Her lips moved as she spelled out the words.

Did they mean what they said?

She looked around for advice. "Hey, mister?" she called. "Can I really have this box? And whatever's inside?"

"Why not?" answered the wizard.

"Terrific!"

Gently, so she didn't shift a single flake from the snowman, the girl eased the box loose and tucked it under her arm. "Thanks, mister!" she beamed. "I can't wait to . . . mister?"

For the subway entrance was empty.

The girl shrugged and turned back to the label. "Guaranteed to come true," she read again. "The Last Wish in the World . . ." She frowned and bit her lip. She had one chance only, it seemed. After that the world would be wish-less.

What should she wish, then?

To be rich?

Or famous?

However hard she tried, she just couldn't make up her mind. Soon her head ached with all the wishes she had to choose from. "This is no fun at all," she wailed. "I wish the Wish in this box *wasn't* the Last Wish in the World!" And she threw the box down on the pavement.

So, hurrying away, she didn't notice that she'd got exactly what she wanted. For out of the broken box slipped wish after wish after wish – all guaranteed to come true. Twisting and turning like snowflakes in the cold night air, they floated across the park and the university, over the streets and the traffic, along the alleys and the shopping arcades, till they filled every highway and every byway in Skyscraper City.

And there, only waiting for someone to discover them, they still are to this day.

MR MIDNIGHT'S TREE BIRD

Sarah Hayes

In front of Mr Midnight's house stood two enormous trees. Every year the trees grew bigger and bigger, and the house grew darker and darker. Eventually the house grew so dark Mr Midnight could not tell whether it was night or day or winter or summer. Week after week he sat in his dark dark kitchen and listened to the wind blowing in his trees.

"Chip chop, chip chop," said the blustery South Wind.

"All fall, all fall," said the cold East Wind.

"Down, down, down," roared the wild North Wind.

But Mr Midnight liked his trees. He didn't want to chop them down. So he sat in his dark dark kitchen and wondered whether it was night or day or winter or summer.

Then the West Wind came – a warm breeze which rustled the leaves in Mr Midnight's trees.

"Cut and clip, shape and trim," sang the warm West Wind.

"Good idea," said Mr Midnight. He fetched his cutters and his clippers and his shapers and his trimmers. And all day long he cut and he clipped and he shaped and he trimmed. Then he sat in his kitchen and looked out. Mr Midnight saw that it wasn't summer or winter:

it was spring outside. Mr Midnight saw that it wasn't day or night, but half-way between the two. Mr Midnight saw that one of his trees was now a bird, all cut and clipped and shaped and trimmed. And Mr Midnight went to bed a happy man.

But the tree bird wasn't happy. She listened to the wind in her leaves.

"Who, who, who are you?" said the blustery South Wind.

The tree bird opened one round eye. She looked at the huge dark shape of Mr Midnight's tree on the other side of the path. She looked at the blackbird roosting in its branches.

"I don't know who I am," said the tree bird.

"Why, why, why are you sad?" said the cold East Wind. The East Wind plucked at the tree bird's leaves and pulled at her branches. The tree bird shivered.

"I don't know why I'm sad," she said.

"Where, where, where are you going?" roared the wild North Wind.

The tree bird knew the answer to that one. "I'm staying right here," she said.

But the wild North Wind pulled and pulled at the tree bird's roots. "Where, where, where are you going?" he roared again. And he pulled the tree bird right out of the ground and whirled her round and round Mr Midnight's house.

"I – don't – know – where – I'm – going," said the tree bird. But she spread out her branches and gathered up her leaves. And suddenly she was sailing up, up and over the wild North Wind. Not whirling round and round any longer, but flying far, far away from Mr Midnight's house.

The tree bird flew all night. When morning
came she stopped beside a little clump of trees. But
she did not stay long.

"You're not one of us," said the great oak.

"You're not a proper tree," said the stately beech.

"You've been clipped!" said the silver birch.

The tree bird flew off, skimming low over the ground, searching
and searching with her one round eye. She found what she was
looking for in the garden of a great palace. The trees in the garden
were clipped into all sorts of fancy shapes. But they weren't very
friendly.

"You're not one of us," said a horse's head.

"You're interrupting," said a tree with a crown.

"You don't belong here," said a tower, and it began to march
towards the tree bird.

The tree bird took off in a flurry. In another part of the garden she found a shining blue bird with a tail that fanned out. But when the tree bird tried to talk, the shining blue bird folded up his tail and screamed at her.

So the tree bird flew away. She flew on and on and on till she reached an old old forest. The old old trees were very kind to her. She nestled under their great branches and hid from the blustery South Wind and the cold East Wind and the wild North Wind.

When she had rested, the tree bird spoke to the old old trees.

"Who am I?" she asked. "I'm not a tree or a bird."

"You're a tree-hen," whispered the old old trees. "Didn't you know?"

"No," said the tree-hen. And she asked her second question. "Why am I so sad?"

"You're sad because you're lonely," answered the old old trees.

"Where am I going?" asked the tree-hen.

The old old trees didn't reply.

Then the tree-hen heard something rustling and singing in her leaves. And she realized that the warm West Wind had come at last. "Go home, go home," sang the warm West Wind.

One day, when Princess Miranda was walking with Molly in the early afternoon, they met a Pedlar Woman dressed in a long purple gown and a cloak of tattered velvet.

"There's something special in my bag today, my little one," she said to Princess Miranda, and she drew from her scarlet basket a length of white satin.

"I'm bored with satin," said Princess Miranda, "and white is a very plain colour."

"This," said the Pedlar Woman, "is no ordinary material. Hang this on a wall somewhere and wait. Something will happen . . ." The Pedlar Woman laughed and the sound was like a white bird calling. "Something strange and wonderful."

"I wonder," said Princess Miranda to Molly, "what strange and wonderful thing could possibly happen to a length of white satin."

"You will have to be patient," said Molly. "Strange and wonderful things take time to come about."

Princess Miranda hung the length of white satin on the wall of the landing. She could see it as she walked along the corridor from her bedroom, just at the top of the flight of stairs that curved down into the hall.

For three days, nothing happened at all.

"I think," said Princess Miranda, "that the Pedlar Woman tricked us. It's doing nothing strange at all. Nothing wonderful either. It's just hanging on the wall like an oversized hair ribbon."

"Shall we take it down?" asked Molly.

"No," said Princess Miranda, "we'd better leave it for a bit longer, just in case."

That evening, when Princess Miranda looked out of her high windows she saw, on the grey ribbon of road outside the castle, a procession of the most extraordinary kind travelling to the strains of a strange, haunting music which went round and round and never stopped. There were elephants and lions, and men in red jackets, and ladies in tights glittery with sequins. There were clowns, and jugglers, and white-faced men in coats patterned with diamonds who could swallow swords and torches flaming with bright fire. There were horses with red ribbons braided into their tails, and on their backs balanced dancers in frothy skirts.

"Come," shouted the dancers and the clowns and all the jugglers when they saw Princess Miranda. "Come and join us!"

"Perhaps yellow," Princess Miranda murmured and returned to her bedroom. As she was fastening the silky bow on her yellow cloak, she happened to glance out of the window. There was no-one on the grey road outside the castle. The procession had vanished and only the faintest echo of the round-and-round music could be heard, blown towards the castle on a stray wind.

"I've missed it!" Princess Miranda cried. "I've let it go by and lost it because I was too busy looking at myself in the mirror. I'm going to go and tear it off the wall and no-one can stop me!"

Princess Miranda ran to the top of the stairs, but the mirror had disappeared and all that could be seen was a length of white satin like an oversized hair ribbon hanging on the wall.

From that day onwards, Princess Miranda looked into the tiny palace mirrors only to see that her face was clean and her hair was tidy, which meant that she was ready to take part happily in everything that was going on in the castle, high on the cliff between the sea and the mountains.

LÉONIE AND THE LAST WOLF

Mary Hoffman

"I'm just going to play outside," Léonie called to her childminder.

"All right, dear, but wrap up warm," Mrs Collins called back. She was busy giving Léonie's little twin brothers their tea.

Léonie pulled on her thick red anorak and her gloves. She put on her red boots too and then picked up a basket she had been hiding in the hall. She wasn't going out to play at all. She was going to visit her grandmother.

Granny Maple lived a bus ride away on the other side of town and she wasn't well. Léonie had heard her parents talking about it at breakfast and she knew they were worried. Back and forth they had talked over Léonie's head, while they packed their bags for work, spooned cereal into the babies and loaded all the children into the car to go to Mrs Collins.

No-one asked Léonie what she thought about it, although she was seven, so she had grabbed a little basket, filled it with what she could and hidden it under her anorak.

Now, standing at the bus stop, she wondered if she had brought the right sort of things for a sick granny. One packet of Liquorice

Léonie looked at him doubtfully. "But aren't you a wolf?"

He sighed. "*The* wolf. The last one in England. Are you scared of me?"

"No," said Léonie, because she wasn't any more. "Should I be?"

"Of course not," said the wolf. "I won't hurt you."

"But why are you the last wolf? What happened to the others?"

"They were all killed. Hunted, shot, trapped, poisoned," said the wolf, looking sadly down his long nose.

"But that's terrible," cried Léonie, and she put her arm round the wolf's neck.

"You are very unusual," he said, nuzzling her face. "Most people are scared of wolves."

Léonie looked at her new friend. "I don't think they'll let you on the bus," she said.

"Then let's walk," said the wolf. "You lead the way and I'll follow at your heels. People will think I'm just your big dog."

So Léonie and the wolf set off down the road to the High Street. It was getting dark and the street lamps were coming on. As Léonie came to a side street, two big boys on skateboards nearly crashed into her. But the wolf leapt in front of her and stood with his hackles up and his teeth bared. The skateboarders goggled at him, swerved and fell off. Then they picked up their boards and ran.

"You see what I mean?" said the wolf. "You are too small to be out alone."

Léonie was glad to get to the brightly lit town centre. But there were other dangers here. Cars drove too fast, honking and screeching round corners. Léonie knew her Green Cross Code but some of the drivers didn't bother to signal. The wolf stopped her from stepping into the path of several turning cars.

At the last crossing before Granny Maple's block, Léonie waited patiently for the lights to change. The snow was falling thickly now and it was quite dark, but Léonie felt warm from the walk and safe with all the people at the crossing and her own personal wolf. Suddenly there was a snarl and a yelp. The wolf had dashed round Léonie and now held in his jaws the hand of a man who was trying to take Léonie's purse from her basket. The other people at the lights realized what was going on.

"Fancy taking a little girl's money! Ought to be ashamed of himself!"

The wolf opened his mouth and the thief disappeared quickly into the snow, holding his wrist.

"Good guard dog you've got there," said an old lady, patting the wolf approvingly.

Léonie stuffed the purse into her anorak pocket. "Not far now," she whispered to the wolf.

Granny Maple's house was right on the main road. It was rather shabby, with the paint peeling off the door and windows. Before she rang the bell, Léonie flung both her arms round the wolf's neck and buried her face in his yellow-grey fur. It was wet with melting snowflakes and smelled of forests.

"You are the best wolf in England," said Léonie. "Even if you are the last."

The wolf gently licked the salty tears from the corners of her eyes.

"I must go now, Léonie. I know how the story of the grandmother and the little girl and the wolf ends. Since I *am* the last wolf, I must be careful."

Just then the door opened and a wedge of lemon-coloured light fell on the path. There in the doorway was Léonie's father. He snatched her up in his arms, kissing her and telling her off at the same time.

"Oh, you naughty girl! We've been so worried about you!"

The wolf slipped out of the light and over the broken wall like a shadow in the snow. Before her father closed the door, Léonie could feel that the wolf had gone.

While Dad went to phone Léonie's Mum, she crept up the stairs and into Granny's bedroom. Granny wasn't lying in bed in a nightgown and frilly nightcap. She was packing a suitcase and wearing her warm winter coat. She hugged Léonie and told her that she was coming to stay with them.

"Yes," said Dad, appearing in the doorway, "we think Granny is getting too old to be on her own. It's too dangerous."

Granny made a little face that only Léonie could see. Léonie thought about how *she* was too *young* to be on her own, and wished

that Granny Maple could have met the wolf.

Dad carried Granny's cases to the car and Léonie and Granny sat inside, eating Liquorice Allsorts, while Dad cleaned the snow off the windscreen. Léonie rubbed a dark circle on her window. Granny's little house looked sad to be left on its own. Then Granny said, "Look at that beautiful dog."

Léonie looked out through her peephole and saw her wolf for the last time. "Can't stand that kind myself," said her father cheerfully, getting in and starting the car. "They always look too much like wolves for me."

Granny turned round to smile at Léonie and winked.

TOMMY THE RHYMER

Leon Rosselson

Tommy the Rhymer bounded down the stairs two at a time. In his stomach, hunger sang a song of soft boiled eggs and buttered toast and in his head, a riot of rhymes danced mazily.

He bounced into the kitchen and stopped short as if he'd collided with an invisible wall. He stood there, staring. Things were not as they were supposed to be. The table was not laid for breakfast. The sink was piled high with dirty crockery. There was rubbish everywhere. In the corner hovered a damp grey fog and through it, Tommy could dimly see his mother slumped in a chair, her head on her hands, her elbows on the unwashed table. She was not smiling. No, she was not smiling at all.

Tommy said: "Mum, you gave me a fright.
The kitchen's a mess. No breakfast in sight.
Why are you looking so gloomful and glum?
And where is your beautiful smile, Mum?"
(You've probably guessed by about this time
That when Tommy talks, he talks in rhyme
Which makes him sound like a bad pantomime.)

"It's no good, Tommy," said his Mum. "I carelessly dropped my smile last night, thinking of something else, I don't remember what, and it broke into a hundred thousand pieces. That's why I'm looking so miserable. It can't be mended. And where will I ever find me another?"

Now Tommy the Rhymer wasn't the sort of lad to be cast down into a dungeon of despair by a broken smile, even one belonging to his mother. He pulled himself up to his full three foot six inches and said bravely:

"I'm sorry you've broken your smile, Mother,
But don't you worry, I'll find you another.
I may," he continued, "be gone for a while,
But whatever happens, I'll find you a smile."

And with that, he went out of the door and into the wide whirling world without even a crust for his breakfast. Truth to tell, he didn't know where he would go to look for a smile and even if he found one, could it ever be as sunlight-on-water beautiful as the one his mother had just broken?

The first person he met was Harry the Hopper, who was hopping from one side of the pavement to the other. Sometimes he hopped on one leg and sometimes on the other but never, ever did he run, jump, skip or, especially, walk.

"Hello, Tommy the Rhymer," said Harry the Hopper. "Where are you going on this semolina pudding of a morning?"

"Well," said Tommy, "this is the position.
I'm off on a very special mission
To find another smile for my Mum
'Cos she's broken her own and she's gloomful and glum.
If you've nothing to do, why don't you come?"

"That's a fizzy idea, Tommy," said Harry. "But where will you look? And do you have to talk in rhyme all the time? It gives me a pain somewhere at the top of my loaf."

"Sorry," said Tommy, "I just can't stop.
I have to rhyme like you have to hop.
Now let's go first to the what's-it shop."

So Tommy ran as Harry hopped down to the what's-it shop at the corner of the street. Behind the counter was Nancy What's-It spreading strawberry jam on buttered toast. Tommy's eyes bulged and his stomach pleaded and such waves of hunger washed over him that his head was jammed with words and none of them rhymed. So he just pointed and opened his mouth like a baby bird. Nancy handed him a raft of buttered toast and strawberry jam and he crunched it hungrily.

"Now Tommy the Rhymer and Harry the Hopper," said Nancy What's-It. "What's it I can do for you this misty moisty morning?"

Tommy's mouth was brimful of toast so Harry, hopping from one side of the shop to the other, answered for him. "It's Tommy's Mum's smile, Nancy. It's smashed to smithereens and she's down in the dumplings so Tommy's off on a mission to find another one. Do you happen to have one here he could have?"

"Sorry," said Nancy. "I've got dandelion soup and bottled toenails and oodles of what's-its, as you can see. Teardrops I have in abundance and I could even do you a nice line in laughter. But smiles are not to be had – no, not for love nor what's-it."

Harry stopped hopping and Tommy swallowed the last piece of toast and shook his head.

"It's not tears I want or toenails or laughter
Or dandelion soup. It's a smile I'm after.
So if you can't help us, we'll be on our way.
I must find a smile by the end of the day.
I think we should try the market square
I'm sure that we'll find a somebody there
Who'll have a smile or two to spare.
But before we go, what I'd like most
Is another slice of jammy toast."

"Here you are," said Nancy handing him a slice or three. "And if you don't mind, I'll shut up shop and join you on your quest. I could do with a breath of fresh what's-it."

So Nancy skipped while Tommy ran as Harry hopped down to the market square where everyone who was anyone was celebrating National Hurrah Day and a seething soup of people heaved and ho'd, shouting and squabbling and scrambling and selling each other blank pieces of paper. And none of them took any notice of Tommy or Harry or Nancy and none of them, not a single pinstripe one of them, wore even the faintest glimmer of a smile.

"It's like trying to hop through a thick forest," said Harry, trying to hop his way through a thick forest of legs.

"It's like trying to skip through a bowl of rice what's-it," said Nancy, trying to skip her way through a rice pudding of bodies.

"Can anyone hear? Does anyone care?
Has anyone got a smile to spare?" called Tommy hopelessly.

But nobody could and nobody did and nobody had.

"Let's climb on the stage at the end of the square," said Nancy, "and then everyone will see us and Tommy can address the assembled multi-what's-its."

So they hop-squeezed, skip-squeezed and ran-squeezed their way to the stage at the end of the square and once on it, Harry did his kangaroo hop from one side to the other while Nancy held up a sign saying:

WANTED – ONE SMILE FOR TOMMY'S MUM
WHO'S DOWN IN THE DUMPLINGS.

And Tommy addressed the assembled multitudes thus:

"Friends and fellow humans, I'll
be brief. My Mum has smashed her smile
And is sad as a cat in the pouring rain
'Cos she thinks that she'll never smile again.
But Tommy the Rhymer, that's me, her son,
Has promised to find her another one
And I will before the day is done.
So friends –" here his voice began to quaver,
"Please hear my appeal, please do me a favour.
Is there anyone here who can do a good deed?
A smile, a smile is all I need
Then my Mum's happiness will be guaranteed."

Tommy stopped and looked down at the thickly peopled square, hoping that someone, somewhere would offer him the gift of a smile. But all he could see were ten thousand blank eyes beamed on him from five thousand blank faces. Then came a whispering like the wind in the trees, then a wailing like the wind in the chimney tops, then a roaring like the wind in hollow valleys. And Tommy and Harry and Nancy saw that the square was packed with people laughing, shaking with laughter, laughing fit to bust, laughing till tears streamed down their faces. But none of them, not a sole single pinstripe one of them, wore even the faintest glimmer of a smile.

From that moment on, things happened so quickly, so suddenly, so out of the blue and the ordinary, that Tommy and Harry and Nancy hardly knew where they were or why. Six burly men in blue uniforms dashed onto the stage and dragged the three of them away. Six slender gentlemen in spotless white uniforms gracefully unrolled a red carpet that completely covered the stage. A carriage drawn by six black horses drew up behind the stage. A spectacular hush enveloped the crowd. An immensely tall man in a scarlet coat strode to the front of the stage and blew three piercing notes on a silver trumpet. Then slowly and ceremoniously, a lady descended from the carriage. She had a gold crown on her head. She wore a white dress. She was smiling graciously.

"It's the Queen," breathed Nancy.

"She's smiling," said Tommy.

"That's what she's paid for," said Harry.

The Queen ascended the red-carpeted stairs to the red-carpeted stage, smiling all the while and waving her white-gloved hand.

"Hurrah! Hurrah! Hurrah!" rose in waves from the packed square for this was National Hurrah Day. Flags were unfurled. A band appeared from nowhere, led by the scarlet trumpeter, and began to play "I'm A Little Teapot", which was the Queen's favourite tune. And through it all, throughout the whole ceremony, not for a single moment did the Queen allow the royal smile to fade from her lips.

As she turned to descend from the stage to return to her carriage, Nancy and Harry were startled to see Tommy wriggle free from the burly uniform who was holding him and race towards the Queen. He reached her just as twelve giant hands grabbed tender bits of his body. The Queen, however, smiled down at him and, with one wave of her white-gloved hand, motioned to the uniforms to leave him be.

Tommy pulled himself up to his full three foot six inches and said bravely:

"Mrs Queen, I know I'm only small
And to you I must seem like nothing at all
But if you could possibly do me a favour
I'll be more than grateful for ever and ever."

And so Tommy the Rhymer told her the story of his Mum's broken smile while the Queen listened smilingly, though once or twice she drew in a sharp breath as if Tommy's terrible rhymes were giving her a pain somewhere at the top of her loaf.

When he'd finished, the surly uniforms crouched on their marks for the order to grab him and charge him with high or even low treason, but instead the Queen smiled and spoke to him and said:

"'Tis true, little loyal subject, that one does have rather a lot of smiles at one's palace, the drawers and the wardrobes are positively overflowing with them, a smile, I dare say, for every hour of the day, every day of the week, every week of the year, a smile, in short, for every occasion. Because in truth, when one is Queen, there are so many occasions, you wouldn't believe how many occasions there are which demand a special smile. But sad to say, these are royal smiles for royal use only to suit royal occasions and they would not do, no they would not do at all for your poor mother. Sorry and all that."

Tommy looked so downcast and disconsolate that the Queen patted his head and (smiling) called for a sheet of royal notepaper, a royal pen and a royal envelope and wrote something on the notepaper and put it in the envelope and handed it to a footman to seal and then handed it to Tommy and said: "This is for your mother, little loyal subject."

And smiling graciously and waving her white-gloved hand, she mounted the royal coach and departed for the royal palace.

Harry and Nancy hopped and skipped over to Tommy.

"You spoke to the Queen," said Nancy in admiration.

"Big deal," said Harry. "Did she give you a smile for your Mum?"

Tommy shook his head mournfully.

"What's that what's-it you've got in your hand then?" asked Nancy.

"It's something," said Tommy,
"the Queen just wrote
To give to my Mum, a royal note."

"I'll hop off home then," said Harry the Hopper. "Sorry you didn't find a smile for your Mum. Never mind. It was fun while it lasted."

"Me, too," said Nancy What's-It. "At least you tried. That's the important thing. Have a good what's-it."

Tommy made his lonely way home through the deserted streets (because everyone who was anyone was still celebrating National Hurrah Day in the market square). It was growing dark now. The day was drifting out of his reach. What could he tell his mother

about the smile he had failed to find for her? Would she be cross and shout at him? Or would she just sit there sadly in a damp grey fog and say nothing?

He let himself in by the back door and went into the kitchen where his mother sat at the table. Nothing had changed since the morning. But when she saw him, she rose from the chair and ran to greet him with open arms.

"Oh, Tommy," she said. "Where have you been all day? I've been so worried."

"I've looked for a smile," he said, "everywhere
At the what's-it shop and the market square
But no-one had any smiles to spare.
Well, the Queen had lots of smiles, it's true,
But they were too royal for me and you.
I'm sorry, Mum, but what can I do?"

"Never mind about that," said Mum, sweeping him up and hugging him. "I'm just glad to have you home again. I missed you and your silly rhymes."

Tommy felt better. He handed the Queen's letter to his mother. She opened it anxiously and read it aloud. This is what it said:

"My golden crown and all my royal smiles for your small son. Is it a bargain? Signed, The Queen."

Tommy's mother screwed the letter up and threw it onto the pile of rubbish. "Never in a million years," she said, giving him another hug.

And there it was, her smile, mended again and beautiful as sunlight on water.